WINGS *of* FANTASY

WINGS *of* FANTASY

A COLLECTION OF STORIES

BY RAGINI BALI

NIYOGI BOOKS

Published by:
NIYOGI BOOKS
D-78, Okhla Industrial Area, Phase-I,
New Delhi 110 020, INDIA
Tel.: 91-11-26816301, 49327000
Fax: 91-11-26810483, 26813830
e-mail: niyogibooks@gmail.com
website: www.niyogibooksindia.com

Text: Ragini Bali

ISBN : 978-81-90193-66-5
Year of publication: 2005
Reprint: 2014

Printed at: Niyogi Offset Pvt. Ltd., New Delhi, INDIA

CONTENTS *contents*

WHAT WRITING MEANS *to* ME

It is so very hard for me to describe what writing is to me. At first, when I was in fourth grade, writing was simply a hobby, something I did in my spare time. But in the middle of 5th grade in New York, I caught the writing bug. Writing became my passion, and the words would flow out from my pen or my keyboard. I felt like a scribe, because I did not compose the words; no, something deeper did, and I was the conduit. I was just the one to write them down.

My writing was shaky at first. I didn't know many spellings. My sentence structure was a dead branch. But I would not give up: I had had a taste of writing, and I wanted to carry it all the way.

But enough about me.

Writing is what constructs my soul. Every person has a special talent that is the food for his or her soul. Mothers' food for the soul is seeing their children grow up famous and educated. Artists feed on bright splashes of colour. For me, it is writing.

Sometimes, something inside of me breaks free of the mortal world, and I am transported to a fantasy realm of my own, where I am a warrior, a princess, or a mere beggar. The line between what is real and what is magical severs when I am writing. When I write, I can make my world as I please.

I have started taking creative writing classes at Leap Years, Vasant Kunj. The one person who has helped me achieve much is Mr. Vikram Sinha. He is my creative writing teacher, and has taught me so much. He has taught me that there is no limit to one's imagination: writers are simply the ones who have the courage to explore those realms.

When I write, my body lies stationery while my soul escapes to joyous places: a lagoon, a forest, or even underwater!

I am what my writing makes me. I know not what drives the force which composes the words in my head; I know not who has truly seen the imaginary places I travel. But ignorance is bliss when it comes to writing: it does not matter if I do not have the answers. There is always tomorrow, waiting eagerly to have a meaning.

What inspires me to write? This I cannot say. Something that touches my spirit and soul, I suppose: that is what inspires me to write. Even though there are hardships, even though I sometimes sob angrily that I could never write and never will, the words make it happen. They drive me onwards. I was always amazed at how small words form a sentence, the sentences form a paragraph, and the paragraphs form a story. And that entire story would not have been possible to make without the tiny words.

Most say that I can write well because I read a lot. That is true. Even in reading, the soul journeys to unknown places, always wondering what's around the bend.

Words are my friends. And to this I say: a man can live without friends: but he can never live without words, verbal or otherwise.

Thank you so very much, Vikram Sir.

The End

MY STORIES

-A COLLECTION

A PIECE *of* MY HEART

On Thursday, February 17th, 2005, something both amazing and beautiful happened to me. Here is the story, the story of the best day of my life.

My mother, my younger brother Raghav and I were at Leap Years, a multi activity center in Vasant Kunj, New Delhi. Here I took creative writing classes and Raghav took computer classes. We arrived at 2:15pm, but our classes started at 3:00. Mama had brought rolls for Raghav and me for lunch. Earlier, we used to stop at McDonald's, but now we eat there sparingly.

Abruptly, I sat down on the green grass. Leap Years has a huge meadow of grass. It felt like the smoothest velvet. I had a sudden desire to roll. So I lay down, and rolled.

The grass held me tenderly. The sun smiled down at me from the ocean of blue that was the sky. I felt free, and I decided to take a risk. I took off my shoes and ran barefoot.

It was sheer luxury. I felt the line between reality and magic disappear, vanish. I leaped, I danced. My heart simply overfilled with pure joy, with love for the simple environment. The grass became a carpet under my feet, the trees massive pillars, and the huge meadow became my mansion: my mansion of nature, of love.

I uprooted weeds with brilliant purple flowers. I talked to the ladybirds, and laughed as they crawled up my arm. I reveled in nature, and its beautiful ability to heal everything. I had exams coming up, but in those 45 minutes, I was no longer Ragini Bali, struggling for a passing grade. I was the one who talks to ladybirds, the one who is joyful. I was a light, carefree sprite. I felt that no fairy could have granted me a better wish, no dream could be more enthralling. And this was real! I rolled in the spring grass, my eyes closed and my heart alight. And near the end, I simply snoozed in the sunlight, dreaming picture-less dreams of joy and laughter.

I woke up and felt the sun's caress, soft and lingering. I heard my mother calling me to go for my lesson. For a moment I had simply wanted to stay in my lovely mansion. Those 45 minutes had felt like only a second!

But I went, and I can still remember my joy. For on that day, I found a little piece of my heart. On that day, I felt pure joy and love - not for any man-made object, but for the simple beauty of nature.

The sunbeams still glow, and the wind still breezes against my face. But I know that I will never have a day like that one again: all the more reason to keep it treasured, close to my heart, which yearns to feel the sun's guiding touch and the grass' soft kiss again.

The End

SONG *of* THE WIND

"As it swirls by,
Forever beyond my grasp.

I heard it sighing,
And uttered a sharp gasp.

The wind is forever moaning,
Forever crying goodbye.

It is always just wind,
Shapeless, and can never die."

THE QUEST *for* TRUTH:

A TEST OF COURAGE

PART - I

He gritted his teeth, refusing to let out the screech that filled his insides. The bushes he was hiding in were low, and thorny. Although there were many bushes, he knew that he could not stay here for long. He must undergo a journey, like the Lady of the Veiled Mists said, to save his queen: and himself.

He heard the great black bird cawing: it sounded like claws being wrenched across a chalkboard. He stiffened, wondering if the bird had heard him. But no; it flew away, still squawking. He heard it mutter, "Must report to Rhita Wvaw, urgent news…"

The soldier froze. Could it be? Rhita Wvaw was the evil spirit that supposedly possessed his queen, Selene. And what was this urgent news? Could it be that the bird *had* heard him?

The soldier knew what he had to do: he had to journey to Rhita Wvaw's castle of death. Only there would he find out the truth. So he readied himself to trek around the Lake of Illusions.

The Lake of Illusions was said to be deadly. Many men saw their hearts' deepest desires, and threw themselves at the water, believing that the images they saw were real. Beyond it lay the Echoing Plains, where the dreams of the people who have died torment the living. Then, the River Warden winds its way through the Quenched Land: where all are suddenly struck by a bout of great thirst. If they drink from the river, their faces turn purple, and they slowly transform into a purple frog. Then, at the edge of the Quenched Land, stood Rhita Wvaw's castle of death: Mvginer. Between the Lake of Illusions and Mvginer there was only one village: he would need to sell all he had brought for food and water.

So began the long trek: the soldier often thought despairingly that he would never make it, that he should just turn around. But always, an image of his beautiful Selene popped into his mind, and he walked on.

One night, when he was nearly free of the Lake of Illusions forever, he saw a glimmer on the lake in front of him. He saw a pale shape glide towards him on silver wings. It was his queen, Selene. Her long, silky golden hair fanned out behind her, and she opened her arms to greet him.

"Oh, Regene, how I have missed you!" the queen cried, her eyes full of laughter.

Regene, the soldier, answered, "So have I, my queen, so have I. But why do you float in the air like a fairy?" His brown eyes held her blue ones, full of love.

"Oh, my Regene, if only you had come earlier!' the queen cried, anguished. "The evil spirit, Rhita Wvaw, killed me yesterday. Oh, what you see now is only an illusion. But jump in, and we shall be together forever." Selene held out her arms, and Regene almost jumped into them. He narrowed his eyes. The Lady of the Veiled Mists had not said anything about Selene being dead!

"But what if the Lady is bad, and Rhita Wvaw is the real good?" a voice hissed in his ear. The two forces battled, but logic won, sense won. Regene broke away from the spell.

"No!" he cried. "You are nothing but a trick! I will not end my life! I will find my true Selene, and I will free her from you, RHITA WVAW!" he bellowed the last words. The image screamed angrily. "Nooooo!" It disappeared in a puff of mist. Regene sighed. It had been a close call.

The Dark Prince of his head still whispered, "You know who the real good is..." But the Light Prince battled back, insisting, "Go on! Brave the Lake of Illusions, and enter the town! Go!" Regene trekked onwards, desperate to rid himself of the doom that circled his head, whispering fear.

Finally, the shimmering expanse of water grew smaller behind him, and a gate loomed above. It read, "Svet de brool Hingarl." Regene entered the village of Hingarl. Inside, thin women stalked the streets, naked children trailing behind. Men with scowling faces occasionally called rude words to each other. The entire place smelt horrible, like a hundred dead carcasses. Regene recognized the smell: fear and hatred.

He knocked at a house that had the word "Marchet" above it. A burly man answered the door, and Regene said that he needed food and water. The man nodded, and Regene stepped into the Hingarl bazaar.

He first bought plenty of provisions, selling his golden buckle, silver helm and long tunic to buy food and water. Then, he saw a horrifying sight as he turned:

Villagers crowded around a pole. Tied to the pole was the most beautiful animal Regene had ever seen: a pure white tiger, with ice blue eyes and silver wings. And the villagers were trying to burn it.

Regene strode to the pole, cut the tiger's bindings, and strolled all the way out of Hingarl, the tiger following him.

Once outside, Regene asked the creature, "What are you?" He flinched as a light voice spoke in his head, *I am Lilypelt Frostclaw, the last of the legendary Cat Warriors. You, Regene, have saved my life: for that, I shall accompany you to your destination. You are a friend.*

Regene saw Lilypelt smile. He nodded, astounded. The Lady had mentioned Cat Warriors, but he never knew that they actually existed!

Lilypelt laughed. Regene recoiled. She growled, *I can read your thoughts, soldier. Beware: it does not take much to turn an ally to an enemy.*

Regene nodded crazily. He must be alert at all times. Lilypelt could be a formidable enemy. He would need her help when he reached the Echoing Plains.

They entered the Echoing Plains that night. Lilypelt shone like a pale beacon as she curled up to sleep. Regene stayed up, afraid of encountering the terrifying dreams. Light and Dark battled, their swords clashing. Light encouraged him to sleep, to endure. Dark cackled that he should stay up. But however much Regene wanted to obey Dark, he fell asleep.

He was lying at the base of a tree. Slowly, painfully getting up, he dragged himself to a large, looming cave, where he limped down a winding passage into the Lady of the Veiled Mists' hidden cave. He threw himself at her feet, sobbing. She silenced him. "I knew it would come to this," said she.

"But I loved her so!" sobbed the poor bedraggled soldier.

"She has removed you because she is possessed, and thinks you are possessed. I have read the tarot cards for you, and they spell a long journey. Go, brave soldier, and find the truth!"

Then there was only darkness. He could not move a bone in his body. There was not a single stir of wind.

Out of the darkness came a whisper of air. It said, "Help me…" He wanted to help the person so badly, so badly. But if only he could move…

"You won't help me?" the voice whispered. "THEN DIE!!!!" it roared. A great, slavering mouth gaped out at him and…

"Regene!"

The soldier woke up. He was sweating, and he felt sick. The dream had done this. But why?

"Rhita Wvaw," he breathed. That beastly spirit! He had sent that dream just so he would get scared and run off!

The swords clashed. "Maybe this is useless, maybe you should leave Selene and go home, save yourself!" the Prince of Dark advised him. But the Light Prince batted him away, urgently whispering, "Go on! Lilypelt is with you. You must save Selene, for not only she needs rescuing. You, too, must uncover your past at Mvginer. Trek on, brave heart!" The cosmic, never ending battle went on, but Regene heeded the Light Prince's advice. He awoke Lilypelt, who growled uneasily. *I do not witness dreams like you humans*, said she, *but I have an uneasy feeling about this place.*

The sun rose and set, yet the travellers were only to the middle of the Echoing Plains. Regene thought that maybe Lilypelt could carry him. Lilypelt threw her head up and yowled, laughing.

Of course, human, she answered. She knelt, offering Regene a ride. He hopped on happily, and hung on tight to Lilypelt's radiant fur.

Flying was amazing! Lilypelt spread out her giant silver wings, and they were swiftly carried upwards by the air. They glided serenely, and Regene marveled at the soft breeze that cooled his hot and anxious face. Lilypelt hummed, pleased that Regene was enjoying the flight.

As the sun began to sink below the hills yet again, Lilypelt and Regene landed in the Quenched Land. Regene was so tired from not sleeping that he dropped off right away, snuggling into Lilypelt's furry side. He was soon fast asleep.

He woke up with a deep desire to drink water. He saw the river sparkling merrily, and crept towards it. Oh, just to have a mouthful of that delicious, silvery water in his mouth!

Regene, no!

Lilypelt crushed him before he could reach the water. "Hey, just let me have some water!" he exclaimed angrily.

Have some from your thermos, then, Lilypelt growled testily. She sounded agitated, and in a flash Regene remembered the legend: he did not want to become a purple frog! "Thanks, Lilypelt," he murmured gratefully. Lilypelt dipped her head graciously.

He took sips from a bottle of water, offering Lilypelt some. She drank the entire bottle. He looked at her reproachfully: now he had only two more bottles of water left! Lilypelt grinned. *Sorry. I won't have to drink again now*, she said.

Regene grumbled. He had some more water before setting out. He could see Mvginer looming darkly in the distance. It would take another day to reach it.

On and on, the two trudged. Night fell, and Regene was sure to have a gulp of water before sleeping. In the morning, he groaned when he saw rain clouds.

"Rain? Why bother? This place is overstuffed with water!" Regene grumbled.

Lilypelt purred. *It is Mvginer.*

So it was: 30 yards away, but in view. Lilypelt knelt.

Care to jump on?

Soon they were in Mvginer, the castle of death, but everything was silent. Lilypelt led Regene to the throne room. There he beheld this horrific sight:

A dark mass that could only be Rhita Wvaw held a woman tied in rope above a...a...no! It was a neth rect, an opening to the underworld. He was going to drop that woman, Selene, into the neth rect!

"Nooo!" Regene threw himself at Rhita Wvaw, but at that moment, Selene dropped. Into the underworld she fell, gone.

"No!" Regene collapsed. "No!" Rhita Wvaw leered above him. He whispered, "You?"

"Me, Regene!" he replied.

"Regene, eh? Well, Regene, I can help you! Only, however, if one life is paid. If one sacrifices, I will send you home, away from here. What do you say?"

Before Regene could say anything, Lilypelt hurtled past and threw herself at Rhita. *Goodbye, Regene! I will never forget you, and we will meet again one day!* She was engulfed by Rhita Wvaw, who cackled. "Mm, your friend had guts, I'll give her that!"

Rhita Wvaw leaned close to Regene. "But Regene, you must know: I am your father. "

I am your father.

Light and dark stopped fighting. Slowly, they fused together. Their colours opened up new, scary worlds for Regene. They were combined. He was Rhita Wvaw's son.

End Part I

THE QUEST *for* TRUTH:

PART - II

He saw a man standing in the middle of a plain, looking around. He looked bemused. A giant lake shimmered behind him. The man looked like he had been in a battle: his tunic was torn, and dirt covered his hair. He was dark-skinned, and tired.

Suddenly, a bird screeched. The man looked up to see a huge black bird. It was a roc, an evil black bird in service of the spirit, Rhita Wvaw. The bird shrieked, and the man darted into a nearby scrub. It was not nearly tall enough to cover him, and the bird spotted a clump of brown hair moving furiously behind the bush. It cawed. Fluttering its magnificent wings, it circled the area, then soared into the sky. It muttered some words, but the most chilling words were, "Must report to Rhita Wvaw, urgent news..."

Regene woke up. His back ached, and his knees were sore. He looked around, and let out a cry of joy when he saw that he was in the Lady of the Veiled Mists' cave. The walls glittered, as though saying, "Welcome back, Regene! Welcome back!"

Regene sighed happily. That entire adventure was just a dream! Just a dream!

"No, my son," a voice echoed in the cave, "it was not a dream."

A lady dressed in fine white lace floated into the cave. Trailing behind her was a lace veil that looked like mist. This was the Lady of the Veiled Mists. She bent down and stroked Regene's cheek. He relaxed.

"Oh, my Lady, it is so good to see you again!" Regene said warmly. Then he absorbed her words, and frowned. "It wasn't a dream?"

"No, Regene. Rhita Wvaw is your father, and Selene is dead."

"Oh, and Lilypelt..." Regene trailed off, anguished. His friend, Lilypelt Frostclaw, Cat Warrior, had sacrificed herself so that Regene could go home. Regene's heart ached as he remembered the white warrior who was so noble.

Then he took in something else that the Lady had said. "Lady, you called me your son?"

The Lady glanced sadly at Regene. He must know the entire truth.

"Yes, Regene," she said. "I am your mother."

"What?!" Regene screamed. "No! You can't be!"

"But I am," said the Lady in quiet tones. "So hush, let us not make a big fuss about it."

"How can I not? I just found out that my parents were the most unlikely candidates ever! You, and Rhita Wvaw!"

"Regene, you must calm down, for your destiny is unfolding. Your future lies at Mvginer, with your father. But remember this line always:

When Dark and Light clash,

One way can Dark be banished.

If the Light can be enveloped by Dark,

Both will forever vanish!

Remember, my dear son, and you will succeed."

As the Lady uttered those words, the room grew dim around Regene. He groaned, lying back. He had experienced traveling like this before, and it was not comfortable.

The brilliant light forced him to tentatively open his eyes. What he saw was unbelievable.

A little man was looking at him with a quizzical expression. The man was two feet tall, and had blue skin. Regene opened his eyes fully and looked around to check that the Lady hadn't sent him to Mars. She hadn't.

"Oh, great savior!" the little man squeaked. "I am Swer, senior advisor to King Qella! But, you see, he has mysteriously disappeared. The scientists tracked him to the great black castle, Mvginer!"

Regene peered at the little man, or Swer. He was quivering, hoping that Regene would help him. Regene nodded his head and got up. "Sure, I can help save your King Qella. But first, let me take a look around."

Regene saw that to his left, looming darkly in the distance, was the dreaded Mvginer. He sighed. Oh, if only he didn't have to go back in!

But, to his right, he saw an army of small blue men, all awaiting his orders. Regene was impressed. These little guys had a very strict training program, that was for sure!

Regene looked once again to Mvginer. The Lady said that his future was in there. So he turned, stared at the little blue men, and barked, "Let's go!"

In order to reach Mvginer from here, all they had to do was to trek across a dry, barren plain for some time. Sounds easy, right? Wrong! The blue men, or Aardaks, had never heard of water or food. They lived simply on microscopic bacteria in the air. So what was he, Regene, supposed to do?

He just walked on, wrestling with his hunger, thirst and pain. The Aardaks could not feel pain. They simply marched behind Regene in perfect formation.

Regene was feeling a little suspicious...

By the end of the first day, they had only travelled one eighth of the plain. Regene flopped down, exhausted. The Aardaks lay down and immediately began snoring. Regene prayed that the Lady would protect him. He half expected a giant roc to screech and fly away to Mvginer, reporting of an army of Aardaks led by him, Regene.

On the second day, Regene felt much weaker. He dragged his feet through the sand. His left foot fell into a hole, and Regene fell: SPLAT! He came up with a mouth full of sand, to witness a rattlesnake slowly slithering towards him. He tried to get up, but his foot was stuck fast. He called to the Aardaks, who were already a mile away, plodding. They had no idea that Regene was not in front of them.

Regene waved his hands helplessly, trying to shoo the snake away. But it came, still hissing softly. It came within an inch of his face and reared. Regene closed his eyes, ready for the killing bite when:

"Hi, are you stuck?"

The snake came closer, waving his tail in a friendly manner. "Sorry about that! The hole you're stuck in was my old hole, but I found a much nicer one. I was just coming to fill it up with sand when I saw you! You looked like a sandman, so I came cautiously. Luckily, you're just a normal human!"

"Are you going to bite me?" Regene asked fearfully.

The snake flicked his tail in an annoyed manner. "NO! For heavens' sake, if I were going to bite you I would have done it earlier! I don't eat meat: I'm a strict vegetarian. Most of us snakes are."

Regene smiled, then winced. His leg was throbbing painfully.

"Uh, Mister Snake, would you mind helping me out here?"

"Name's Sammy, and sure! Now you just lie still, and I'll have you out in a jiffy!" Sammy crawled into the hole. Regene could hear him loosening the sand, making the hole bigger. After some time, Sammy crawled slowly back out. "Well, you're leg's free, but do you ever wash? Your foot stinks!"

"Thanks for the tip, Sammy," Regene grumbled. He gingerly pulled his leg out and saw that it was purple and swollen: badly. He groaned. "Now what am I to do? I was supposed to help those Aardaks get to their king…"

"Whoa, did you say Aardaks?" Sammy asked.

"Yeah, so?"

"Oh, man! I'd better tell you then," and Sammy whispered into Regene's ear. Regene nodded grimly. "I somehow had a feeling," he said somberly. "By the way, Sammy, you got anything to patch this up?" Regene motioned to the swollen leg.

"Sure thing, buddy," Sammy answered. "These." He tapped his fangs. "They carry healing poultices, get it? All I have to do is insert one into your leg and it'll be as good as new!"

"No way!" Regene said, horrified. What if Sammy's fangs carried deadly venom?

"Relax, it'll be over in a sec." Sammy quickly inserted a fang into Regene's swollen leg. Regene screamed, but he saw his leg heal before his eyes. It flattened, and it looked like there was never any swelling!

"Wow, thanks, Sammy," Regene said, awed. He waved a goodbye. "Gotta go now: I'll keep in mind what you said!"

"You'd better!" Sammy called. He flicked his tail, and slithered away.

Regene kept up the gruesome trek, but somehow Sammy's fang had quenched his thirst, cured his pain and satisfied his hunger. So Regene went on, thinking about what Sammy had said. Somehow he had always known. But now he was positive: the Aardaks were not who they pretended to be.

After a horrible, four day trek, Regene arrived at the gates of Mvginer. To his surprise, he saw a golden sword lying on the ground next to the gates, engraved with his name: Regene. He picked it up, and found it was light. Confidently, he walked into the palace.

Again, it was empty. The last time he had been here, both Selene and Lilypelt had died. He did not have happy memories of Mvginer.

Regene walked to the throne room, where last time he had seen Rhita Wvaw holding Selene, his love, above a neth rect, an opening to the underworld. As Regene watched, Rhita Wvaw released Selene, and she fell. But this time, Regene was not surprised.

All the Aardaks were assembled in front of a dark mass that was Rhita Wvaw, evil spirit supreme and his father.

Regene remembered Sammy's words: "The Aardaks are creations of Rhita Wvaw! They are leading you to him!" Regene had felt suspicious about the Aardaks, how they kept walking on all the time. Now he knew it was because they were Rhita Wvaw's minions.

Regene stepped into the room. Rhita Wvaw turned. He held a silver sword in his hand. Regene stood firm, and called, "Rhita! I am here to challenge you!"

"Well done, Swer," Rhita smiled. "You brought him here!"

"Yes, and now, let us fight!" Regene said.

Rhita Wvaw responded by bringing up his sword. He brought it down, only to have Regene deflect it with ease. Regene channeled his anger at his father into his sword, where he slashed mercilessly at Rhita Wvaw. But he could not even wound him. Regene was desperate, when a voice floated through his head: *When Dark and Light clash, one way can Dark be banished. If the Light can be enveloped by Dark, both will forever vanish!* The prophecy! The Lady had told him this, and he now understood: in order to banish Rhita Wvaw, he must sacrifice…himself. So he lunged, sword pointed at Rhita Wvaw's evil being, and allowed himself to be swallowed. He heard Rhita scream, and as he moved into the darkness, Rhita Wvaw faded to light. They both disappeared, changing to one another. Regene met his beautiful Selene and Lilypelt in the Underworld, while Rhita Wvaw was banished forever to the Dark Pits, where spirits who have abused their power slave for the rest of eternity.

So Regene found where he was truly supposed to be: among his loved ones, forever. And he tells himself that if he relived his same life, he would never change a single thing.

The End

EEATY

eeaty

Tzel. Hello. My name is Dorm, the star. But I am residing on Earth now, and here I am called Ragini. Let me tell you of my travels:

I paced, or rather, glided, from one wall of the house to the other. My body sat in a chair, listless and glassy-eyed. I could take many forms on Eeaty, my home planet, but I preferred being free, not limited to a physical body. My thoughts scrambled, sliding everywhere. I stopped abruptly.

Someone was at the door. As thoughts cannot open doors, I regretfully slipped back into my physical form.

But wait. I could not. I was being blocked: being blocked by a powerful source. I was hurtled back as I tried to slip into my body. I could always pass through the walls: physical forms, however, cannot.

I glided silently through the wall. Two seconds later, I wished I hadn't. For the streets were dark red, stained by physical and mental blood. Forms lay screaming, dying, while bright thoughts slowly faded until they were nothing.

Evil. Something evil had done this.

I could not bring myself to look at the poor bodies and souls that lay dying. So I focused on something else: what the source was.

I soon located it: a dark wave, engulfing everything and sending out rays of fear and death. Evil ruled Eeaty now. I could not stay.

I fled upwards, seeing my beloved home shrinking, until I had reached space and it was nothing but a round ball.

I wept mentally, releasing my anguish to the other planets in waves. I stayed there for a time, then went on.

I continued until I could no more. I landed heavily in a brown wasteland: a planet called Slatin. I collapsed, my thoughts all in disarray, and my mental body aching.

I lay down for I do not know how long; I drew memories of my happy times on Eeaty, of the flowers, of the blue skies, of the peace I had felt there.

"No!" I told myself savagely. "You will not think these thoughts! You can never return there!"

Unfortunately, I didn't feel any better.

A while later, a green blob walked, or slithered, up to me. It bore three eyes, and five arms. It had no mouth, yet I heard its words clearly: "You must go to Earth, third planet from the sun in the galaxy Milky Way."

I nodded, but I forgot that he couldn't see me. So it rolled its three eyes and disappeared into Slatin's monotonous brown surface.

I mulled this thought in my head. Earth: never heard of it. Of course we had heard of the Milky Way: ulsa vre danska Spedbirkes erk cochoyets gin danlos. (I mean: they make the best speedbikes and chocolates in the universe!)

"Earth. Gond ga," I whispered to myself. (Earth. Nice name.)

I set off towards the Milky Way, which was in the west. Stars twinkled merrily, and I was once again reminded of Eeaty. Each of those stars was a million miles away, but they had life on them. No evil had invaded them, I'll bet. Otherwise they would be blackish balls.

I travelled at the speed of light, being whisked in the currents of light. I was headed for the Milky Way, and Earth.

I was pulled past many stars and planets, most of which were light and bright. I sighed, longing for Eeaty.

After not much time, I was brought in sight of a blue-green planet. Earth.

As I descended into the atmosphere, I felt a sharp pain. My thoughts must enter a physical body. I screamed, the pain digging into me like a red-hot dagger, branding me. I took the shape of an infant girl.

So now, I am called Ragini. I have gotten used to Earth life, even to the extent that I call it fun. But part of me will always long for Eeaty, and the carefree life I led there.

The End

FRAGRANCE

fragrance

Diana sighed. She was the basic storybook princess: waist length black hair that smelled of dew; deep, dark blue eyes which sang of untold knowledge, of both the past and the future; rose pink lips which yearned to talk, to chatter with another human. Her skin, the colour of oak, was smooth and smelt of jasmine. And she was locked in a high tower.

Her father had put her here. Before his wife, the Queen Piara, passed away, she whispered words into her father's ear, soft as the wind through the trees. Diana still did not know of the words. As for the story: she had smelt it.

Diana had an amazing sense of smell. She had discovered it...yesterday. She had been looking out the window when this story of her mother flowed into her head, liquid and smooth like water. She had pulled away, startled, but soon leaned her head back out. It had rained last night. She smelt the joy of the earth and smelt the wheat grow yet taller. She smelt the crystal dewdrops on a rose, and she smelt a message from the trees in the wood: "Come hither, Princess.. "

Diana rejoiced at the little freedom she had. Today, when the sun was rising, she had smelt the weariness of the sun, of slogging through the sky. When the sun itself rose among the pink and golden mists, Diana smelt its joy at seeing the world so peaceful.

Yet Diana did not only smell joy. Far away, she smelt terror. She smelt the heavy, overwhelming stench of blood. It made her cry out, when the smell of blood laced through her nostrils.

And, most peculiar of all, she smelt fear : fear from her father.

Diana looked down, and saw the velveteen grass gleaming in the sunlight. The grass called to her, "Come! for a way out comes. You shall be free before the sun sets."

Diana turned to the woods, eager to smell messages from the trees. But they were silent today. The river flowed, and Diana smelt a strong burst of fear, of hatred: no more.

Now, the fear loosened, vanished. Diana smelt a noble presence in the woods, but she could not decipher what it was. So she turned yet again to the palace, where she hoped to catch her mother's dying words.

She smelt the usual attention, strictness…evil? Yes, so it seemed. A reeking smell crept towards her from the Minister of Agriculture's room. In her mind's eye, Diana saw the minister posing proudly. She heard him say, "Ha! I will pose as a prince to rescue that princess, Diana, from the tower. Then, I can use her powers for my own benefit! As the Queen said, she has a sorceress' powers!"

Diana stepped back, shocked. How? She could not have powers! She could do nothing special, except, except…

Her sense of smell.

That was the tool! That was her power! So Diana put her power to full use. She sat on her silken coverlet, and she sat for 100 years. The coverlet rose, trembling. She swayed back and forth, smelling a fresh, sharp fragrance. Someone was coming closer.

The coverlet landed back on the bed. From Diana's swaying, it twined itself. It grew, and grew, until it was a long rope. And at that moment, Diana opened her eyes. She felt weak.

For she had just seen the future if the Minister of Agriculture rescued her. Children lay crying on the streets. Dogs fought each other for food. And the roses, her precious roses, were limp, dead. Their crinkled brown petals formed the dismal atmosphere.

And suddenly, each falling petal became a portal! Diana had stepped through one, and the room came back. She sat, shivering. Then she smelt a fragrance as fresh as spring, and looked out of the window.

There stood a man, with pale blond hair and green twinkling eyes, that seemed to be a giant, yet was a million miles away. For he was a prince, struggling through the woods. But Diana saw him at the bottom of her tower. She saw the rope on her bed, and, securing one end to a hook near her window, she threw it down.

It was not long enough! She then smelt the sun. It sang, "Reach, Diana, reach!"

Diana pushed. The rope dropped a little lower. She thought of the earth singing wordless songs after rainfall. The rope crept down. She thought of the wheat, edging its way into existence. The rope fluttered down. She thought of the majestic sun, crowned in halos of pink and gold. The rope was almost there!

Then Diana thought of the pink roses, dripping with dew that looked like pearls. And the rope dropped into the hand of the stranger! Diana opened her eyes. She saw that she was in the woods, and that same man, gentle and patient, kneeled beside her. She knew that all the time, she had been reaching for her freedom. And now, she had it. The world smelt like the fragrances of roses, dew and spring, all mixed together into an unearthly, celestial perfume.

She was free.

The End

the VISIT

Mr. Edkins felt nervous. He noticed that the large garden, normally busy with maids and bees, was empty. The flowers seemed dull, too. With great regret, he knocked lightly on the door. There was no answer.

He proceeded to open the large, heavy door. He stepped into the house, the house he had not entered for 19 years.

Mr. Edkins had hurried over as soon as he had heard that his father was sick. Although he had left him at the age of 16, he was still concerned about his father. And when a man visiting his little town mentioned that a certain Frederick Edkins was fatally ill, Mr. Edkins had set off.

Now here he was, waiting for someone to either bring him the happy news that his father had recovered, or for someone to sorrowfully tell him that his father was dead, or dying. But no one came. The entire house seemed empty of people.

Mr. Edkins walked up the steps of the large Victorian mansion. In 2000, houses like these were rare. His father, now at 80, had bought this house 40 years ago. Mr. Edkins, at 35, had lived here until his father, a widower, had started trying to get married again.

So he had left. But now, Mr. Edkins trekked up the stairs. He reached the first floor, where he automatically strolled into the library.

From a young age, Mr. Edkins had always had a passion for books. So his safe haven was naturally the Edkins' library.

The books still piled high, but now the room had a musty smell. Mr. Edkins, however, spotted an ancient-looking black book on the table near the door. It was about the size of a diary.

It had his father's name, Fred Edkins, on the front in curly gold letters.

Mr. Edkins opened the book. He read the first heading, "6th June, 1932." This *was* a diary, his father's diary when he was twelve years old!

Mr. Edkins started reading:

6th June 1932

Today, I was sitting by the river running by the village like a snake. I like to put my hands in the cold stream water and feel them tingle.

Frank, the poorest boy in the village and an orphan, approached me. He tentatively said, "H-hi, Fred, c-can I s-sit next to you?" I shrugged and then nodded.

Frank sat down next to me, and gazed at the river flowing by. He turned and spoke.

"It was all such a long, long time ago. I suppose I could be angry, looking back, but I'm sure they meant to do their best for me… and now, I haven't the heart to be bitter."

I urged him to go on. "What is it, Frank?" I asked him curiously.

"Oh, I was talking about my parents," Frank sighed.

"But you said that they were killed when you were 5 months old!" I said, horrified. It was true.

"I was lying. They…they… they abandoned me!" he burst out, sobbing. He crumpled, and I moved to comfort him.

"No, don't bother," he said. "I just want to tell you what happened."

"I was five, a year younger than when I came here. Mum and Dad had started to quarrel, I don't know what about. But they would never look me in the eyes, and our relationship, which had once been loving, grew faint."

"One day, when I was sleeping, they left me on the side of a road and fled. First I searched for them, but I could never find them, not even the slightest hint."

"So I came here, well, actually, I stumbled across your village. And here, I was given to a family that loved me." There were tears in Frank's eyes.

I patted him awkwardly on the back. "Uh, don't worry, Frank, we're here for you," I said. Oh, real smooth. I'll bet he's really feeling better now!!!

Mr. Edkins looked up from reading. This was odd: his father had never told him this story before. He usually told his children all of his childhood stories.

Mr. Edkins read on:

22nd August 1932

Today some new people came to the village. They had a lot of cool things, like light produced in a small, confined space! They were trying to convince one of us to go back to their…city with them. I desperately wanted to, but I knew I never could.

They told Mrs. Wellington, the chief of our village, that she didn't treat her chickens properly. Yet they never did anything. They just lounged around. I've always wanted a little free time.

When Mrs. Wellington saw the strangers eating all our last autumn's harvest, she lost her nerve. Actually, she had lost it a long time ago: I think this was the last of her nerve. Handing me her broom, she got herself into a proper rage, until she was almost puce in the face.

Mrs. Wellington was boiling with rage as she marched across the yard towards the visitors.

"You people…you people! You make me sick! You come here to our village – tell us how to look after our animals…you've never even got your feet muddy before, I'll guarantee!"

The strangers looked quite taken aback. "You can leave now!" said

Mrs. Wellington. "I think you've tried to corrupt enough of us!" The visitors echoed one more plea. "Please, will one of you come back with us?"

"I should say not!" fumed Mrs. Wellington. But I had made my decision. "Yes," I found myself saying, "yes, I will come with you."

Mrs. Wellington stood awestruck. The visitors seemed pleased. They took my hand and asked, "How old are you, my boy?"

I replied nervously, "I–I'm twelve, sir."

"Oh, you must go to school! We will put you in 7th grade," the man said.

"Please, sir, what's school?"

The man laughed.

As our carriage rolled out of sight, I heard Mrs. Wellington screaming, "Fredrick Edkins, don't you dare ever enter this village again!"

Mr. Edkins dropped the book in astonishment. His father had actually once lived in a village? But he picked up the book and avidly started to read again.

19th November 1932

Do you realize, diary, that it has been nearly four months since I have come to London, in the city? The village, I have learned, was the west of someplace called York. But here, I have joined a basketball team, but we are horrible. Jo, our team captain, nearly shouts herself hoarse every practice. She is in 9th grade, and considers us all inferior. She issues so many extra practices, that sometimes I cannot finish all of my homework! The teachers are also very frustrated with me, but they cannot punish me as I do all of my work: well, most of the time. And when I do it, I do it well.

Diary, I had the nicest dream the other night. We had just won the Championship Cup in Basketball (CCB) and Jo was still stunned. She hadn't said a word to us yet.

Jo turned to us, her team. "You did it...you deserved everything you got because of your hard work! You won the Cup, and played some of the best basketball I've ever seen…and I knew you would, from the moment the game began!" She was actually praising us instead of shouting at us and lecturing us!

Ah well, I suppose I'll always have my dreams.

Diary, I feel lonely. During break, no one comes to me and offers to trade lunches. No one wants to play something with me.

But, luckily, I still have you, Diary.

Mr. Edkins was still shocked. All these years, his father had lied to him. He had talked about living in London all his life, when he had really only come here when he was twelve! He had lived in a village!

But nonetheless, tears gathered in Mr. Edkins' eyes. He felt an immense sorrow for his father, striving to be someone. He felt like he was 12-year-old Tom Edkins again. His father had longed for the exciting city life, while he, himself, wanted a peaceful country life.

A maid rushed in. "Oh, Master Thomas," she burst out sobbing, "oh, your father: he's gone, he's passed away. But before he went, he smiled and said faintly, 'He knows the truth now.'"

Mr. Edkins bent his head mournfully. Although his father was a liar, he was his father and he missed him. He wished he had a chance to say goodbye.

"Master Thomas, in his will, Master Fredrick left you the house." The maid had dried her tears. "Will you be taking over, then?"

Mr. Edkins' head came up. He knew he had to look after this house for his father, and for the mother he had lost a long time ago. A sense of peace and calm-mindedness enveloped him.

"Yes, maid, yes. I am here to stay," said Thomas Edkins.

The End

the PRISONERS

The cells were dark and dirty. Flies buzzed drunkenly around the place. The steel bars of the cells had fingerprints from numerous prisoners screeching and pulling at the bars. The floor, made of cold, gray slate, had stains of porridge and gruel, where men had thrown their precious meals in a tantrum. Whenever a bell rang, the cell-in-charge would walk up to one lucky person's cell, unlock it, and lead the bedraggled prisoner to meet whomever had come to see him or her, while others shrieked protests.

The prisoners themselves were a dreary bunch. There was Pat, a 17-year-old girl who had been caught trying to murder an old lady. There was Sam, who had had drugs and killed someone. There was a maniac, Derek, who wanted to take over the world. He would mutter incoherently to himself, but when he let out a maniacal laugh, everyone else shouted at him to be quiet.

And there was Betty. She was only 10, and orphaned. Betty was apparently caught stealing, and since she had no parents, she was put here, in prison. But Betty had not stolen anything: she was a sweet child, with golden hair and brown eyes. She was not used to the hardships of prison, and cried every night.

There were many more dismal prisoners, all grouchy and eager to rid themselves of Hightop Prison, Alabama, once and for all; I could go on forever. But these four are the important ones.

One night, Betty sent up a wail. Pat, who was jealous of this little child, screamed at her to be quiet. Pat had dark skin, greasy red hair and weak gray eyes. She wore glasses.

But Sam felt pity for this little girl, who had done nothing wrong. So he, Sam, a fat 22- year-old with brown hair and blue eyes, shushed the little girl. "Ssh, Betty, you don't want to put the cell-in-charge in a bad mood, do you? Ssh, there, there, Sammy's here," he crooned. Betty fell silent, enjoying this man's humming. She whimpered once, then slowly crawled into her stiff bed, where she fell asleep.

Sam felt his blood boil. This little girl should not be here! She was still a child. How cruel the law was! For Sam had fallen in love with Betty, who was so innocent, and who only voiced her pain at night. In the day she was a cheerful little creature, always looking to brighten someone's day.

Derek, however, was sleeping deeply. He was dreaming that in his very cell, he had discovered the cure for the common cold. So the guards were forced to release him, and all the other prisoners were staring at him and shouting, "Not fair!"

Derek smiled in his sleep. Ah, if only dreams could be reality!

Pat was angry. Little Betty always got all the attention! And Betty would probably be released soon; after all, she had only *stolen* something! Pat decided that when she got out of jail, Betty would be the first one she would murder.

Betty, however, was having a dream where Sam was her father and Pat was her mother. Pat convinced Sam to abandon Betty, and they left her on the roadside, crying. Betty shivered.

Sam tried to sleep, but his mind was disturbed. He wanted, more than anything, to free Betty. The little girl deserved to see life to its fullest. He fell asleep, frustration tearing at his brain.

Derek had woken up. Encouraged by his dream, he peered around the cell. There was only an empty porridge bowl, but Derek held imaginary chemicals in his hands and mixed happily.

Pat still could not sleep. After her decision, she lay down. But she could not go to sleep. Pat wondered if it had something to do with Betty. In a rush she realized that she did not hate Betty; she loved her, loved her with all of her grudging heart.

Betty smiled at Pat, in the cell across. She really wasn't so bad, Betty decided. And, miracles of miracles! Pat smiled back.

Derek sighed. He slumped on his bed. He could never discover the cure for the common cold. He wept silently, then perked up. Only six months more, then he could resume his plan to rule the world!

Sam smiled at Betty and Pat. "I think we are all going to be the best of friends," Sam said to himself.

And Betty and Pat agreed with him. Derek only cackled, but then again, he was crazy.

The End

UNDER *the* SEA

I Watched the sun sink slowly below the horizon. It threw its last rays on the ocean, making it shine like gold. Each ripple was clearly defined, and with the setting sun it looked like a dream.

I sighed and dived into the waves. Luckily, way out here in the ocean, I don't have to worry much about Humans seeing me.

Now you may ask: why would you not want a Human to see you? Well, the truth is, I am a seahorse. No, not one of those itsy little things, but a literal seahorse. My hide is pure white, my mane and tail aquamarine. I have a golden horn, so you could say I am a sea-unicorn. My name is Seasilk.

Under the waves, the sea is the most beautiful place known to the Earth: gently moving turquoise waters, colourful plants at the seabed and most of all, merpeople. We sea-unicorns are sometimes owned by merpeople, but not I. I am as free as the sea itself. I go as I please. I live my life daringly, always trying. Those sea-unicorns who prefer an easier life can have it; I'm not interested.

Yes, it's true we must hunt for our own food, eating little fish or plants. But that constant difficulty is repaid by knowing that you can depend on yourself to do what you want. You feel independent: proud. And rightly so.

Although the sea is lovely, it has many dangers too. Sharks the size of… what do they call them on land? Oh, yes, *trucks,* prey on sea-unicorns and other things. Crabs as big as islands also feast on us, and a sea serpent is devouring us. Sea-unicorns are growing rarer and rarer, and merpeople are hungry for the remaining ones.

And, surprisingly, so are Humans.

One slightly forgetful mare, Snowtail, swam to the surface during warm-waters. A Human spotted her, as she is pure white and the waters are bright blue. He started shouting, and Snowtail grew startled. She dived back into the waters, and she didn't come up again. It wasn't her fault; she was born with a slight memory loss.

Now, whenever one of us mentions the surface, Snowtail shudders. Poor thing.

Seasilk swam among the turquoise waves, her bright white coat gleaming as the sunlight filtered through the water. Her horn glowed, and her deep brown eyes twinkled. Tossing her head, she was the perfect picture of wild beauty.

The hilly regions around the Merking's palace have the best seaweed in the ocean! I swim there often. The merpeople are normally asleep when I graze.

But today was different.

While capering happily through the colourful flowers, I failed to notice two merwarriors, clad in armor, lurking around the hills. With a warcry they sprang on me, two long ropes in their green hands. Quickly, efficiently, they bound me down. Turns out they're not warriors of the Merking, they're deserters. Simply, it means that they left Merking Triwent and sold their services to Humans. So, I was really in trouble.

Roughly dragging me, they swam towards the surface. In cold-waters, the surface is unbearable. Luckily, I can breathe above water too. Otherwise, all the Humans would get were dead sea-unicorn carcasses.

One of the merwarriors grinned, showing me black teeth. I shuddered. With a hoarse laugh, he prodded me with his metal pike. Metal! Under the sea there is no metal. I see it occasionally when I swim above the surface. The metal must have been these merpeople's payment. I flattened my ears and hissed. How dare a merperson sell me to those barbaric Humans for metal!!

They hauled me to a small wooden rowboat. In it sat a horrific sight: a leering, fat bulky blob that turned out to be a Human. He smiled at the two deserters, and gave them a pile of metal weapons. I hoped they were all counterfeit.

The Human poked me fiercely, laughing. I didn't understand what he was saying. Chuckling, he threw himself at the oars and the boat creaked, slowly moving. I wondered how it moved; the Human was so fat!

The ropes were tied around my legs and neck. But none were on my face, so I lunged and gave the blob a nip. He bellowed in pain, like an animal. I smiled in satisfaction. But the bite seemed only to enrage the blob even more; he paddled furiously until he reached the shore. That meant only one thing: land. I can walk on land, obviously, but the hot ground hurts my hooves. I prefer the cool waters. Even though it was cold-waters, the sun is stronger on the surface than it is in the ocean.

The blob muzzled me firmly, tying the thick rope around my face several times to form a crude halter. I shivered, feeling his fat, podgy hands prod me. He laughed again, hoarsely. He yanked me violently, and my muzzle smarted. Covering me in a white sheet, he pulled again and I followed him blindly into a…yes, truck, where he stored me like seaweed in the back, snickering all the way to wherever he was taking me. The white sheet was soon a mangled mess, but the blobby Human only chuckled even harder when he saw the remains of the sheet. This time, the sheet was tied to me rigidly, and again I tagged along behind him, thoughts raging through my brain. The biggest question I had was: why me? Why couldn't the merwarriors have captured some other sea-unicorn? But I hurriedly reprimanded myself for this kind of thinking as I was led inside a building. I could tell it was a building because it was much warmer here. A stallion, Blackwing, had been captured by Humans during cold-waters and he had said that the Humans had devised a system of heating indoors. For once, I was glad there were Humans. The warmth was welcoming, although the sea is also quite warm. When the sheet was removed from my eyes, I was amazed.

I was in a tank about seven times my size. It was filled with warm water, and a pile of seaweed was in one corner. It was a huge tank, but I felt trapped.

My mane felt dull. I felt sick. Humans came and *oohed* and *ahhed* over me. And about two weeks later, the blobby Human dropped something else into the tank. At first I didn't realize it was another sea-unicorn. Then I sniffed unenthusiastically and found out that he was a male, from the tribe of Seaworth. I am from the tribe of Bluesharp. There are about twenty tribes of sea-unicorns in the ocean. Each tribe holds about 50 sea-unicorns. That's how rare we are.

I turned to greet him and gasped. He was dark blue, with a silver mane and tail. His green eyes were cheerful. His horn was of crystal. To my utmost horror, I felt my knees weaken. This sea-unicorn had already swept me off my hooves.

In a cheery whinny, he said, "Hi, I'm Skyhorn. So nice to meet you."

I heard myself whisper, "I'm Seasilk."

He whickered and I found the courage to ask, "Skyhorn, why are you so happy that you are trapped by Humans?"

He grinned. "Well, because I have such a pretty companion!" I blushed. He was flirting with me!

His face clouded. "It is nice to meet you, Seasilk, but right now we need to get out of here."

I nodded, strength returning to me. "But the Humans guard us at night, when there are no other Humans."

He threw an admiring glance at me. "Right! So we need to figure out when there it no one here."

His green eyes glowed, and I suggested tentatively, "What about midday? The place is empty, and the Humans are off eating." Skyhorn nodded. "But it'll take some time to think out a plan," he whinnied. "We can't leave for some time."

I nodded again. Skyhorn seemed so sharp, so in control. I was in love with him already. His razor-sharp green eyes picked up every little detail. I also tried to scout for ideas, but it was so hard. When seaweed was dumped into the tank, Skyhorn was quiet, munching his share slowly.

Two weeks from when Skyhorn first came, he nudged me awake one night. "Awake, pretty lady," he said, smiling. I flushed again. He knew how I felt about him! He said, a little more softly, "I've figured it out. Today, when the Humans are out eating, we will jump out of this tank."

"How? It's too high," I said. He beamed, nodding his head. "Yes. But you, Seasilk, can climb onto my back. You jump out, and leave."

"I can't leave you here, alone!" I cried. I felt very strongly for Skyhorn, and I couldn't leave him behind.

He smiled sadly. "I'm afraid you must," he said quietly.

"No! I won't! I…can't," I said softly.

"Why, Seasilk? We are of different tribes. We should not care what happens to each other. I can survive here. Why can't you leave me?"

I looked into his green eyes, as green as grass. And I whispered, "Because I love you, Skyhorn."

Skyhorn's green eyes shone. He gently touched his muzzle to mine and said, "I love you, too, Seasilk. But we can never be together. You know that."

"But we can at least escape together!" I cried.

"How, Seasilk? How?"

I had an idea. "Why don't we escape three nights from tonight. At night there are Humans, but you've seen how sleepy they look. We won't eat for those three days and nights. They give us seaweed twice a day, so the pile of seaweed will be very high. I can jump out first, then you can."

His green eyes gleamed. "Yes, you've got it, Seasilk!" he cried. He pressed his flank against mine, and I felt warm. I murmured, "We'll get out of this together."

Three nights from then, we were both weak with hunger. Skyhorn gasped, "No, Seasilk, you must go. I can stay here."

"But knowing the Humans, they'll kill you for letting me escape!" I said. He gazed at me so tenderly that I lowered my head, embarrassed. "We will escape together, my love. We can do it," I whispered. Skyhorn responded by leaping over the glass walls of the tank, landing effortlessly on the other side. He waited, and I gathered all my nerves and prepared to jump.

Just then, a yell was heard. There was only one Human guarding us, and he had been fast asleep when Skyhorn had leapt clear. Now he was lumbering to the tank, his shapeless hands stirring the air everywhere.

Skyhorn bravely faced him, and with one swift lunge, he pricked the Human's skin. The Human instantly fell into a deep sleep. I had forgotten that even sea-unicorns have magic.

I jumped over the glass wall, the soaring feeling of flight still with me as Skyhorn and I raced across the city to the harbor. With a graceful leap, we were in the fresh water. Immediately we dived under the surface, and as we swam towards the ocean floor, I felt that one visit to the surface and shore was enough. Never again would I venture there.

I took the lead, guiding Skyhorn to the camp of the Bluesharps. My mother, Aarabele, sprang up. She had not yet seen Skyhorn.

"Oh, my daughter Seasilk!" she whinnied joyfully. "I had lost all hope of ever seeing you again. Thank the Sealord you are back once more!"

I cleared my throat nervously. "Mother," I said, "there is someone I'd like you to meet."

Skyhorn stepped out from behind me, and he was greeted by

outraged whinnies. "That's a Seaworth unicorn, that is!" "What is the meaning of this?" "Seasilk! Have you changed tribes?"

My mother hushed them all. With loving eyes, she asked me softly, "Seasilk, will you please explain?"

"Skyhorn and I were both captured by Humans," I began. I told the silent tribe about our adventures, and how our love blossomed. "I would like to take Skyhorn as my mate," I finished. The tribe was still hushed, until an old gray sea-unicorn came to the head of the group. In a hoarse voice he said, "If love is pure and strong, there is no harm in it. And if I know the sea, then I know that Skyhorn here is the Prince of Seaworth!"

I looked at Skyhorn, amazed. He grinned sheepishly. "I was afraid you wouldn't want me if I told you I was a Prince, or you would only love my money," he said softly.

I pressed myself against him. "Skyhorn, no matter who you are, I will always love you," I whispered.

The old one continued, "This union will join the Bluesharps' and the Seaworths' land, which have not been one for nearly 500 years!"

One mare asked, "Do you approve, old one?"

The old unicorn smiled. "Yes," he said, "I wholeheartedly approve."

Now it is three years later. Skyhorn and I are still steadfast mates, and we still love each other as we did the day we first met. Now we are joined by three little foals; Blackstar, a completely black colt with a golden horn, the oldest; Firespark, another colt who has a red hide, golden mane and tail and an orange horn, middle; and finally, my sweet Seascamper, the only filly with a white hide like mine, a golden mane and tail, sapphire eyes and a crystal horn.

We are a small family, but we love each other. And if you are by the sea, then listen! You may be able to hear us playing.

The End

MISTFALL, LAND *of* MISTS AND DREAMS

Whenever I close my eyes, it comes to me: Mistfall, my realm of fantasy. Where my friend, the unicorn Seasilk, rules as Princess and I am a warrior. With my keen silver sword at my side, I travel Mistfall's outer regions, wary for any sign of trouble.

Shrouded in mists, Mistfall is a solitary, fertile island adrift in the middle of the Crystal Sea. Named after the legendary crystal of power, which supposedly lurks in its depths, the Crystal Sea is home to sirens and merpeople. The sirens sing alluringly each night, but the citizens of Mistfall are immune to their sweet songs.

Unlike what most foreigners think, Mistfall is actually quite big. With four to five large towns scattered around the island plus the elite town where Princess Seasilk's palace is found, Mistfall has quite a large population. Due to a forest thickly surrounding the island in a protective ring, Mistfall is the ideal sanctuary for many mythical creatures, some rarer than others. Unicorns and dragons roam the forest. One small female dragon called Zira is Her Highness' First Councillor. Wolves also howl on stormy nights. Once, there was even a manticore wandering in the forest!

Let me tell you about one of my adventures in Mistfall, where my warrior name is Tigereye. This one is called "The Mystery of the Manticore":

"Warrior Tigereye! We need your help!"

I was in Mistfall, where I am the sole warrior. Zira, First Councillor to Her Highness Princess Seasilk, was fluttering around my head, agitated. Zira is about the size of a full grown terrier. She is a small dragon, but nonetheless trustworthy and true.

Zira screeched into my ear again; "We need your help!"

I swatted her away angrily. "D'you want to make me deaf or something?" I yelled at her. She simply hung in the air, shocked. My bad moods do not come often in Mistfall.

So in a gentler voice, I asked her, "Zira, tell me, what is the matter?"

"I think I can answer that for you," a sweet voice said. From the next room stepped in Princess Seasilk, Her Royal Highness, a unicorn. She fixed me with one brown eye and whinnied quietly, "Supposedly, a manticore is on the loose in the Dark Forest." The Dark Forest surrounds the island of Mistfall.

Zira trilled frantically, her squeals getting more and more annoying. But I didn't want to hurt her feelings, so I tried to bear her hysterics.

Her Highness' white coat gleamed and her aquamarine tail and mane cascaded magnificently. Her golden horn glowed. But the Princess was not a docile creature; if provoked, she was a formidable warrior. Her horn was like a great sword, only better as it could not be knocked away from her. When in battle, her placid, gentle eyes burned with fire.

I whistled for Aniu, my wolf friend. She padded into the room, her golden eyes shining. Her long white coat was the colour of snow. Aniu was special; I was bonded to her. She could read my thoughts, and I could read hers. I buried my face into her coat and whispered, "Come, my wolf warrior; destiny calls."

Aniu instantly knew what the problem was. Her eyes smoldered as she growled in my head, *Do not worry, Tigereye. If it hurts you, I will hunt it down until I kill it*. I felt reassured. Aniu never went back on her word. She and I were truly bonded, as an animal of Mistfall and a human should be. Even the lowest farmer had a bonded mate; if the bonded animal should die, then the bonded human would, too. I gazed into Aniu's golden eyes and was glad that she would protect me.

My silver sword, Deathsong, quivered in its sheath. It had been nearly three months since it had last tasted the blood of an enemy. I squared my shoulders and nodded to Zira. She flew hurriedly out of the room, and I followed her.

Outside, a massive silver bird with strange black markings waited. In the outside world he was Lugia, a Pokemon. But here, he was his true self; Silverwing, the legendary bird of Mistfall. Silverwing nodded at me, and Zira huffed. She squeaked, "Silverwing will take you and Aniu to the spot where the manticore was last spotted. Your job is to either kill it or drive it off Mistfall. Good luck!"

I jumped lightly onto Silverwing's vast back. He hummed, speaking like Aniu, *I am happy to be of service, young warrior*. I braced myself, and Silverwing soared into the air.

No beast could fly as high as Silverwing. Not even the dragons, who were double his size. Silverwing was truly the Lord of the Skies and the Seas; he could dive underwater and not surface for two months. I cringed, not daring to see how high up we were. Aniu, however, was thoroughly enjoying the ride, the wind whipping her fur everywhere. I felt a combination of joy and exhilaration coming from her. She seemed to be despondent when the ride was finally over. Silverwing nudged her and hummed, *You will get a special ride after you defeat the manticore*. Aniu nodded, her tail wagging. Loyally, she trotted into the forest, her nose scenting everything. I followed her, mistrustful of the surroundings.

Aniu suddenly let out a sharp bark, which translated itself as, *I smell blood! And meat!* I dashed through the thick foliage to her side. With horror, I saw a torn carcass of a black bull, its blood still soaking into the ground. By the look of utter contentment on the bull's face, the attack must have been both swift and stealthy. And it was fresh.

Aniu picked up the scent from the bull immediately, but paused, flicking one ear uneasily. *This smell is vaguely familiar,* she growled. I did not have her superb sense of smell, so I put all my trust in her. She was my partner; together we died or survived.

The scent trail twisted and turned; obviously the manticore was trying to throw us off. But Aniu had the best nose in all of Mistfall. She doggedly continued, despite the fact that she was gasping for air. Finally, the scent led to a large cave, certainly large enough to fit a manticore. Aniu lay down, exhausted by our "little run".

From the cave came a soft crooning. I drew my breath in sharply. This must be a manticore! Manticores were known to sing softly to their victims, then pounce on them and finish them off!

I edged closer to the cave and sniffed. Instead of the smell I had expected; rotting meat, the stench of death, I smelt…hay. I smelt hay, roast beef, chicken, woodsmoke…My head whirled. This could not be a manticore. Manticores do not know how to cook.

Aniu lifted her head and smiled. *Yes, young warrior, you figured it out; this is not a manticore*, she barked softly. I stroked her, and she licked my cheek. *Go on, and take Deathsong with you. It will protect you. I'm afraid I can't do that much just now.*

I fingered Deathsong, and I felt its power surging through me. Confidently, I strode to the cave entrance, but stopped. From then on, I crept silently down the coiling passageways. I could smell the fire and food more strongly now. I was getting closer…

Then, ahead, I spotted a large entrance through which light gushed. Singing echoed from the cave, and the overpowering smell of food made my mouth water. I peered into the cave, and drew my head back in astonishment.

A musician, tall and agile, was sitting among a horde of treasure.

Satin cushions and finely woven tapestries surrounded him. He had a fire going, and was cooking beef above it. A little further away, a black hide lay next to several knives. The bull! He must have killed it, then torn away the succulent bits of meat with his other knives to make it look like a manticore had eaten it. I felt rage claw at my heart. How dare he? He had probably demanded payments from the village folk in return for the safety of their cattle. He was playing a wooden flute, its tunes becoming a soft whisper at the beginning of the passage.

I clasped Deathsong firmly and leapt into the cave. The musician looked startled, and I quickly bound his hands with a bit of his own rope. I tugged sharply at the rope, and he mechanically followed. I led him all the way back to the entrance of the passage, where Aniu stood waiting. She grinned, growling approvingly, *Well done, young warrior. You have caught him*. Together we walked back to where Silverwing was waiting for us. He whistled in astonishment when he saw us with a miserable looking musician instead of a manticore. He didn't ask any questions, though, of which I was glad. My fury was bubbling fast, threatening to overtake me. Aniu bit me gently, and I tried to control my thoughts into a more positive lane.

The Princess congratulated us when we showed her the "manticore". The musician regretfully told the truth; that he was poor, and needed food. Her Highness banished him to the dungeons for a year, saying, "You could have come and told me. Most villagers do have a problem, and they come and talk to me about it. I always help them, but I cannot help you. You are too deceitful for words." The musician hung his head shamefaced.

Zira nervously praised Aniu and me, but she was a little preoccupied. Another case had been brought in; a farmer's neighbor had supposedly stolen his cows. Zira's ruby eyes pleaded, but I shook my head. I had to return to the outside world. As I opened my eyes in bed, I heard Aniu's voice softly whispering, *I will be with you always, young wolf warrior*. I smiled contentedly.

The End

SHADOW *in* THE MIST

It was a new moon. The mist hung like a shroud around the little bay. Tranquil waters lapped softly against the silver beach, sliding silently. In a small thatched hut by the sea, a little girl slept. Sleeping the sleep of the innocent, she dreamed on.

Suddenly the waves churned. There was no wind. The girl awoke with a start. Glancing about nervously, she tiptoed out of the hut. She crept down to the coast, and what she saw made her dive behind a rock.

Her breath shallow, her heart pumping, she stole another glance. Her eyes widened in wonderment. For among the misty waves was a ship. A glimmering, pale ship it was, too pale to be real. From it came the clanking of chains and the moans of unfortunate people.

The sand felt cold beneath her feet. It was December; it was bound to be cold. But the girl shivered. Her pale silvery hair blending with the mist, she stared at the ship, half in excitement, half in wonder and terror. On the highest mast flew a black flag; a sign of pirates.

That evening, her grandmother had told her the story of the ghost ship. "Your great-great grandfather had gone to fight the pirates," she had rasped, a wild glint in her fevered eyes. "He defeated 'em, and brought their treasure here. It was mountains of gold, piles of jewels, oceans of silver! And it's all supposed to be buried right here! However, legend has it that it is cursed."

"Cursed how, Grandma?" she had asked curiously.

"Cursed so that if a soul touches it, will die instantly."

Her grandmother's robe had flown around her wildly, and her hair had whipped into her face.

"Is it true, Grandma?"

"Yes! And we'll all die; the pirates will hunt us all down..." her grandmother had cackled.

Now the girl heard chanting coming from the ship. She crept closer, her pale face ablaze with excitement. She could see a tall man on board, with his back turned to her. He had long, dirty yellow hair. She drew her breath, and the man turned.

She nearly screamed. He had the palest face she had ever seen! His dark, empty eyes spotted her, and in a hollow voice he called, "Wait..."

She took off, flying over the sand. She raced to her grandmother's hut, jumped hurriedly into bed and waited breathlessly. When no one followed, she slowly relaxed, dropping back into her deep slumber.

When she awoke, soft sunlight filtered through her window. Her grandmother was calling, "Gwen! Get up, you lazy! There's work to be done!"

Gwen slowly got up. Her mysterious turquoise eyes glowed. They were not mesmerizing eyes, but deep ones. You could read her feelings from her eyes; her hunger for food, being the smallest of a family of seven; her wariness of her eccentric grandmother, yet her joy of visiting her; the pain of her grandfather's mystifying death, four months earlier...

Then Gwen remembered the previous night. Had it been a dream?

But the sand between her toes said no; she had been out last night.

The day dragged on, Gwen eager for night to come so she could visit the ghost-ship again. When she finally went to bed, she could not fall asleep. She listened for the singing of the ghost pirates. Soon it came.

Again, she slipped out stealthily. Again she hurried down to the coast. As she thought of meeting the ghost pirates, she said out loud, "Bobby would have loved this." She remembered her red haired, brown-eyed brother with a grin. She boldly trotted to the eerie ship and called, "I must speak with your captain!"

The same long haired man came. He looked at her and chuckled in the same hollow voice, "What spirit you have."

Gwen was overcome with curiosity. "Why is your voice hollow?" she asked.

The pirate captain laughed. "We're dead."

Gwen suddenly remembered her purpose for coming down there again. She challengingly said, "Why do you have to haunt our fair shores?"

The captain laughed again. "For a young 'un', you sure know a lot of words, but you are a stupid girl," he said, glaring at her. "Because our treasure is hidden near your house!"

Gwen remembered the story. Of course! So she bravely said, "If I help you find your treasure, will you go away?"

"Yes!"

The silver shores echoed with the captain's reply. He added, "I'm Coldstone, by the way."

The next day, Gwen had completely forgotten about her promise to

Coldstone. She was happily digging in the sand, a few feet away from the hut.

Suddenly, she unearthed a faded black book. It was small, and had thin writing inside. Gwen was seven years old, so she knew how to read. She read the golden words on the cover: "Samuel Q. Reound".

Reound. That was her grandfather. Gwen fervently opened the book and began to read:

1st August

Found a HUGE mound of gold today. Must be the lost treasure Grandfather found. Will not tell Clara about it. My poor wife needn't worry herself stiff. Covered it with sand.

2nd August

Felt a little queer today. Took some medicine and felt better.

Gwen read in horror as each day her grandfather's health grew worse. She was disgusted to find that her Grandpa had kept such an important secret from his wife.

In the last entry it said:

I know I must die tonight. I feel terrible for keeping such a secret from Clara. So I will place my diary on top of this horde, this cursed horde. Goodbye, world.

Gwen was horrified. The curse! But it all made sense. Grandma had found him dead in his bed.

Gwen shuddered. She must tell Coldstone about this diary.

That night, Gwen told Captain Coldstone that she had almost found the treasure. "It will be with you tomorrow night," she said, startled at her own boldness. Coldstone, however, nodded approvingly.

The next day brought howling winds with it. Barefoot, Gwen dug up the mountain of gold, her eyes stinging from the sand that flew about. She sat down with a sigh. That night she would transport it to the shore. She only hoped that Coldstone would keep to his part of the bargain.

The winds howled terrifyingly that night as a little girl deposited six piles of gleaming gold and shining jewels to the shoreline. She yelled, "I've got your gold!" The wind snatched the words from her mouth, screaming them across the vast beach. Coldstone lowered a huge basket.

"Pile it in," he ordered.

When the treasure was all aboard the ship, Coldstone gazed at Gwen. Another man came to stand with him. Gwen choked back a cry. It was Grandpa!

Coldstone said, "Gwen, you have brought us our treasure back. Thank you. We will leave, but first we would like to ask you to join our crew. Will you?"

Gwen thought about all the things and people she would miss, like her mother and father and siblings. But she looked into her grandfather's eyes and saw immense pride there. He inclined his head very slightly. Gwen lifted her head up and declared, "Yes, Coldstone. I will join your crew!"

Her grandmother found her body the next day by the shore, a small smile on her pale lips.

The End

THE ADVENTURES *of* STEVEN DREEL

THE TRUTH OF IT ALL

PART - I

In a little inn on Elliot Road, in the grassy plains west of London, there lived a man and his wife called Mr. and Mrs. Pumbletrook. They were the innkeepers of the Rusty Home, a nice, cozy little inn. They had four floors; the bar was on the bottom floor, the guests' rooms on the second and third floors, and Mr. and Mrs. Pumbletrook's rooms on the top.

There were seven rooms on each floor, and one windy, black night, Room 2-6 had an unexpected visitor.

A screech of pain awoke the Pumbletrooks. It had come from Room 2-6. Plump Mrs. Pumbletrook hurried down the large marble banister, while skinny Mr. Pumbletrook followed at a slower pace.

The door to Room 2-6 was agape. The furniture was scratched, the bedsheets all over the place. And in the bathroom, where moonlight from the ornate stained glass window gently caressed his pale face, was Walter Harvey, who had checked into Room 2-6 the previous day, 17 March 1784. He was dead.

Instantly, Mr. Pumbletrook dived for the telephone. He automatically rang up the most famous detective in all of England: Steven Dreel.

The next day, Dreel arrived in a horse-drawn carriage. His black hair hung limp, and his face was red.

"Yes, is this the Pumbletrooks' inn?" Dreel said. "I am Steven Dreel, at your service." He bowed stiffly. The Pumbletrooks quickly explained what had happened last night.

"Let me first inspect your guests," Dreel puffed. He sank into a red armchair, taking a few minutes to regain his composure.

"Ahem, yes. Lead me to Room 1-1!"

Room 1-1 housed a man called Peter Schyole. He came from Norway, and his glasses gleamed in the early morning light, hiding his gray eyes.

He shook his pale hair out of his eyes. "You is not murderer, I hope?" he quavered.

"No, Mr. Schyole."

"O-o-okay, c-come in," Schyole stammered. He pulled the heavy, oakwood door to reveal Lion's feet.

Lion's feet on everything. The drawers, the closet, the bathtub, the sink: all resting on heavily polished bronze lion's feet.

Schyole himself had a very odd appearance. He wore baggy trousers, but a crisp collared orange shirt. His shoes were scuffed, and he looked very tired. Though his room, with the gleaming Celtic designs and rich mahogany paneling was spick and span, something about it made Dreel feel uncomfortable.

"Thank you, Mr. Schyole," Dreel said loudly. He stepped out, not before noticing Schyole's expression change from meekness to cunning. There was definitely something very odd about this man.

Dreel turned and bumped against someone. As he apologized, he realized that the someone was a woman.

She had glossy black hair, fern green eyes, and a teasing smile. "No need to apologize, Mr. Dreel," she said musically, "or shall I say, Detective Dreel?" She laughed, the sound of wind gently tinkling crystals. "My name is Maeve Forrest. Allow me to show you my room."

Maeve led Dreel to Room 2-1, up the white marble banister. She opened the door with the numbers "2-1" engraved in gold, and at first Dreel just saw a clock carved with angels around its rim. Then he saw the elegant chairs, the small bed, the applewood walls, and a design of vines on a wooden plate, propped against the mantle. Dreel did not expect anything to be there, but on closer observation, he saw that small letters formed ~~W+M=Mrs~~. As you can see, the writing had been scribbled on.

Apart from the scribble, everything else was clean and shining, with some comfortable armchairs, but mostly hard backed wooden chairs. There were cabinets made out of oak, and the table was made of ash. There were little colourful cushions scattered everywhere. The cushions stood out even more, as everything else was either white, black or gray.

Maeve gathered food from some cabinets. Her green gaze locked into his as she asked, "Oh, please, would you join me for some lunch?"

Dreel looked at Maeve, in a dark green blouse and black skirt. He felt like relaxing for some time. "Sure, why not? But I must tell you, I'm here on research. You know Walter Harvey was murdered last night, so I'm here to investigate. But," he added as Maeve's eyes widened, "I can surely stay for lunch with you, Ms. Forrest."

"Oh, please, called me Maeve," she replied.

"Maeve, then. I was going to go to the nearby diner for some food, but that doesn't sound so appealing now," Dreel said.

Maeve nodded. "Oh, I have plenty," she said. "Besides, diner food is not at all nice, and the nearest diner is at least a mile away."

Dreel sat on a chair as Maeve moved around, graceful as a swan. She strained some spaghetti, and started to cook it. Then she made a tomato sauce, loaded with fragrant herbs and some chilli. It smelt delicious, and Dreel enjoyed Maeve's company. When they sat down to eat, Maeve asked him about his earlier cases, and listened intently as Dreel related them. When at last the food was finished, Dreel got up and said, "I must leave now. May I have the pleasure to meet you tomorrow, maybe for a late dinner?"

Maeve laughed. "Of course," said she. "See you tomorrow, at 8pm, in here. Bye!" She waved as Dreel walked out, and he felt regret at going.

As he walked down the banister to the ground floor, he ran into the Pumbletrooks again. "Excuse me, but what time did Maeve and Peter sign in and when?" he asked them.

"Oh, Maeve's only been here since last evening. She checked in at about 5:20, I'd say," Mr. Pumbletrook replied.

"And Peter's been here about a week," Mrs. Pumbletrook added. "Came in at 7:30am sometime last week." She frowned, her displeasure of the Norwegian man showing.

"Well, mind if I take a peek at the other rooms?" Dreel asked.

"Oh, don't bother looking at Rooms 1-2 to 1-5," Mrs. Pumbletrook said. "The Greers family lived in those rooms: there were twelve of them. They checked out last evening."

"Actually, on the entire first floor, there are only Peter and a man, Mr. Sleeny Fluer, who lives in Room 1-7," said Mr. Pumbletrook, surprised. "I didn't realize it until Mrs. Pumbletrook said the Greers had moved out."

"Well, then I'll check Mr. Fluer's room." Dreel strode to Room 1-7. He knocked on the door, but only an echo answered him. Dreel pushed open the door, and the sight that met his eyes was astonishing.

The room was empty. The green brocade curtains were torn and fluttering. The ornate gold-framed window was open. The armchair in the left corner of the room was dilapidated, its upholstery torn. The giant four-poster bed in the middle of the room was missing its drapes and two legs, so it sagged at an odd angle.

Dreel rushed up the banister, and turned the doorknob of Room 2-2. It was locked. He tried the same with the other doors, but they were all locked. With the exception of Room 2-6: where Walter Harvey was so cruelly murdered.

Dreel looked at Harvey's face, and realized that the look on it wasn't pain: it was pure joy. And a small pink mark left by lipstick lingered on his cheek, colliding strangely with the small round hole above his heart where a bullet had ended his life.

As Dreel looked down at the out of place expression on Harvey's face, he asked himself angrily, "What person that Walter Harvey loved so much could bring themselves to murder him? *Who?"*

End of Part I

THE ADVENTURES *of* STEVEN DREEL

THE TRUTH OF IT ALL

PART - II

Dreel ate dinner with the Pumbletrooks silently. He was still shocked at the fact that someone Harvey loved actually murdered him. After a dinner of rice, mashed potatoes and beans, Dreel curled up on a mattress on the floor of the Pumbletrooks' living room. He was soon fast asleep.

The next day, Dreel got up stiffly. For a moment he had no idea where he was. Then, in a rush, all of his clues came back to him: the locked doors, Sleeny Fluer's empty room, Peter Schyole's sudden change, the writing on Maeve's plate…

It must seem to you, dear reader, that the murderer was one of the visitors behind the locked doors, or Sleeny Fluer and the Greers family, who both fled. It could be any of them…or none of them.

Dreel was quite sure that he knew who it was. But a good detective never accuses anyone without evidence. So he set out to find some.

He started by sitting quietly under the great marble staircase, reading a book on bees in the dim light. But his mind was on the staircase above him. Two minutes later, he was rewarded with the sound of soft footfalls above him.

Dreel slid out just in time to see Schyole turning a corner on the third floor. He followed the pale man to Maeve's door.

Maeve opened the door with a smile. However, it was not a smile Dreel was accustomed to. It was a sad and regretful smile. She whispered, barely audible to Dreel, who was flat against Room 2-2's door, "Come in, Schyole: it has been done already." Peter Schyole slipped in, and Maeve closed the door behind him.

Dreel knew that either Harvey was murdered by a woman, or a woman was present at the time of murder. So he had to find out how many women there were in the inn. Maybe one of the occupants of the locked rooms was back, and was a female.

Dreel paused by Harvey's door. He peered into the bathroom, then went closer to see if he was right.

He was right. There was another man lying next to Harvey. He had brown hair, a beard, blue eyes and a dark face. And he, too, was dead.

Dreel looked closer. Now, he noticed that Harvey was clutching a photo.

Dreel gently removed the photo from the dead man's hands. When he looked at it, he almost dropped it in amazement.

It was a photograph of Walter Harvey and Maeve Forrest! Maeve was resting her head on Walter's shoulder and was laughing. Walter was tucking a purple flower into Maeve's raven hair. They both looked so happy, and the picture was no older than a year, for the faces of the two had not changed.

And a note was attached: "I am still yours, even if you can never be mine."

Dreel mentally put the pieces together. Writing, Peter's face, Mr. Fluer's open window…

"So," a voice spoke behind him, "you figured it out."

Maeve stood behind him, with Peter at her side. Maeve was holding a gun, pointed straight at Dreel's heart.

She laughed bitterly. "I loved him, Steven. I truly did. I gave that man my heart and soul, and what did he do in return? He cancelled our marriage plans so that he could travel to Asia! But I kept on loving him. Until that love transformed to hate, and when I met Peter here," she motioned to Schyole, who grinned, "I set out to kill him."

"But I could not kill the man I still loved, with a little part of me. So I sent Peter to kill him. I, however, came back to say goodbye. But then Fluer found out, and I was forced to track him down and kill him."

"And now you, Steven Dreel, will be the third to die because one man could not care enough about me!"

Dreel found his voice. "No," he said.

Maeve lowered the gun and laughed. "No? Why?"

"Because if you loved Walter, you would own everything up. No, Maeve, there will be no more killing."

Maeve collapsed with a sob. "No," she cried, "no more. I wish for no more!"

She laid down her gun, but Peter snatched it. "Are you mad, Maeve?" he hissed. "He must die!" And Schyole picked up the gun, breathed, and pulled the rusted trigger.

That was the last breath of Peter Schyole. For as he pulled the trigger, the gun backfired. The needle sharp bullet hurtled itself into Peter's throat, and he died instantly.

Dreel looked at him, regretful. "You could have made something to be proud of, had your mind not been corrupted by deceit. Now you have paid the final price: your life."

The police sentenced Maeve to twelve years of prison.

Maeve became a news reporter. But that would be another story. As for the Pumbletrooks, they had business aplenty, as men wanted to seek shelter from the wives they had left behind.

The End

RUNNING *with* THE DEER

A BEAUTIFUL MEMORY

The doe looked at me with her soft brown eyes. Her little fawn squealed, begging for more milk. But the doe kept staring at me, ignoring her fawn. As I looked into her dreamy brown eyes, I felt for a second that she and I were one. But the connection vanished as she bounded away.

That day was lovely. I saw many deer at this nature park in Jabalpur. But what really made it special was that doe, who had a splotch of white streaked across her muzzle.

The bucks, with their proudly raised heads and velvet antlers, stared haughtily at me. The fawns, naughty little things, played games with blades of grass. Most of the does seemed snobbish. But my doe, whom I decided to call Tara, (star) crept slowly up to the fence once more. We locked eyes again. I felt a rush of unexplainable joy.

My Naanu hurried me back to the car, with my Naani and my brother, Raghav. I continued to watch Tara until her delicate head disappeared.

I often wonder now about my Tara. Was she old? Was her fawn grown up now? Was she dead? But I will always remember my Tara as a slim, beige doe with big, brown eyes.

Tara and I made a bond that day, but I have not seen her since. But Tara is what made that memory beautiful, for I felt then that she now belonged to me, but I belonged to her, heart and soul. Tara is the star that lights up my life.

The End

NIGHTMARE *on* ELM STREET

SHORT STORIES

Four children walked into a dark, rickety house. Each held a brightly coloured marshmallow in his or her hand. The confident, dark girl with black hair, who was on the porch held a bright sky blue marshmallow; the calm, demure girl with brown hair, trailing behind, had a calm orange marshmallow; the jumpy, excited boy who was hopping up the steps had a vibrant red one, and the boy who had a mischievous grin on his face carried a purple one. These four children pushed open the heavy door, carved with picture of eyes, and walked in.

The brown haired girl flinched as the door creaked shut behind her. She whispered, "Guys, I don't think this is my house."

The black haired girl looked at her. "But you said your house was on Elm Street!" she exclaimed.

"I know, Sally, but I just remembered that it wasn't Elm Street, it was Oak Street," the girl said apologetically.

"Ooh, Samantha, why didn't you say so earlier!" the boy with the red marshmallow groaned.

"Well, sorry, Jake, I just remembered," Samantha said defensively. Jake rolled his eyes.

The boy with the purple marshmallow spoke. "Why don't we just leave?"

There came a click. Samantha gulped. "Because, Dave, someone just locked the door."

the GOLDEN DEER

Old man named Gustav: There is a wonderful story of the golden deer and how many people from all over the world wanted to catch the deer. Except no one succeeded.

Little boy named Marco: Is it true that there is a golden deer in the Forest of Mubawar?

Gustav: Of course!

Marco: Rubbish! I don't believe that the coat of the deer is actually made of gold.

Gustav: The fur has the shinning colour of gold and it is said that in the navel of the deer there is a nectar called Kusturi.

Marco: Then I will go and get it.

Gustav: Oh no – no you won't! You don't know that there is an illusive wizard called Gomez who guards and protects the deer. It is not possible for a child to go there and capture the deer. For the nectar Kusturi is important for all wizards and magicians for their many magical deeds.

Marco: How do you know?

Gustav: I know – but that's it! You're not going!

Marco: Well, what if you went with me? You seem to know a lot about the golden deer and Kusturi and Gomez.

Gustav: Ah, yes. But I suppose you could go if I came along. But first, I need to tell you the story of the deer: Long, long ago, a little deer stumbled into the den of the mighty bear sorcerer, Solomon. Solomon was astounded at the deer's courage, so he turned its coat gold. But at a cost: he placed his powerful nectar, Kusturi, into the creature's navel. The deer never knew, and was puzzled why so many strange men came chasing after it. It always ran away from them, until a powerful wizard, Gomez, offered his services to the deer. So Gomez keeps the deer safe, but every night he slits its navel, collects some nectar and seals it back up. But it is known that if half of the nectar is taken, the deer will die and the nectar will be spread to all parts of the world, but Gomez doesn't know it.

And that's the story.

Marco: Wow, the poor deer. But surely Gomez has taken more than half of the nectar?

Gustav: No, no. Each night, the nectar disappears from his cup and restores itself into the deer's belly. You see, the nectar must be used in some way within 6 hours; otherwise, it will return to the navel. Of course, the wizard doesn't know it.

Marco: Then how do you know it?

Gustav: Never you mind. Now, we need to pack. You, boy, pack food and a few personal belongings and meet me back at the first tree of Mubawar Forest at 6.00 in the morning, okay? It's starting to get dark now.

Marco: Okay.

(The next day)

Marco: I got my things.

Gustav: Good. Now, let's set off!

The two explorers stepped into the forest, where they were immediately swallowed by darkness and fog. Even the trees seemed to push them away, warning them not to step further. Sometimes Marco made as if to turn and run, but he always grudgingly turned back, as Gustav would stop for nothing.

Marco: I say, Gustav, can't we take a break? My poor legs are killing me!

Gustav: Now you listen here, boy. Aren't you the one who wanted to find the deer so badly?

Marco: Well, yes, but…

Gustav: No buts! You have to give something to gain something. Don't you know?

Marco: I don't care. I'm sitting down.

Marco sat down, while Gustav plodded ahead, his mind on the deer. Presently, a soft rustling came from a bush behind Marco. A small golden figure stepped out. Marco gasped. It was the deer!

Marco: You're the golden deer!

Deer: Yup, I am. The one who's always running away. Say, how come you're not chasing me?

Marco: I did want to catch you, but you're so beautiful that I should like to have you as a friend. Do you agree?

Deer: Sure, if you won't chase me. Why does everyone chase me, though?

Marco: Because you have this really powerful nectar inside you called Kusturi.

Deer: Oh. And by the way, that old man you were with? He's Gomez. Did he capture you or something?

Marco: No, he told me his name was Gustav.

Deer: The usual. Had you not fallen behind, he would have led you to his fort, told you I was in there, and locked you in there to starve. Geez! Last week he was Michel.

Marco: Do you feel a sudden urge to leave?

Deer: You bet!

Marco: If we leave, can't Gomez follow us?

Deer: Nope. Contract says that when I'm out of the forest, he can't leave it. He thought I'd never leave, so he agreed. And the contract's magical: he can't break it.

Marco: May I ride you?

Deer: Sure, why not?

So Marco and the deer left the forest for good, leaving Gustav/Gomez furious. Marco only took a sip of Kusturi, but now he and the deer live forever. The deer, called Shimmer, is Marco's best friend and closest companion. Marco and Shimmer often relate the tale to each other, and each remembers the howl of fury that followed them back from the forest; the howl of Gomez, forever trapped in his own wood.

The End

a WAVE HAS HIT

NEWS REPORT BY RAGINI BALI

The earth gave a slight shudder. The oceans near the tip of India churned. And seconds after, the wave arrived.

The giant wall of water moved at a frightful pace, crashing into India's southern coastline. It took Sri Lanka along on the ride.

Soon, another wave came, but it was not a monster. This wave gently washed ashore the remains of houses.

The southern coastline of India, along with Sri Lanka and parts of Central Asia were devastated. Only poor fishermen lived on the extreme coast of India, and in a span of 45 seconds, they saw their lives' work being washed to sea.

Mothers found their still infants. They cried, wept, screamed. How could they not? The wall of water, or as the Japanese call it, the tsunami, had taken their little babies. Men found the broken, scattered remains of their houses. All in all, India mourned.

We asked some scientists for their theory of how the tsunami happened. Most said it was caused by and underwater earthquake, but some others thought that maybe a new island had surfaced, or was going to. This tragedy took place on 26th December 2004. It is now 14th February 2005. No island.

The fact is clear though: many parents lost their beloved children, and many children lost their parents. Animals were found dead as well.

The fishermen need our help. Many people are generous in contributing money.

The astounding thing is, the tsunami has actually changed the entire earth! The axis is more tilted, there were snowfalls in humid Dubai, and grass actually grew in Antarctica!

Although the tsunami has cost us many lives, and changed our earth, it has given us a gift, too. It has taught us that we Indians must help each other, especially the less fortunate. When the sun rose on 26th December, no one knew that on that day, a shimmering wall of water would destroy many lives. No one knew that corpses would be washed ashore in great numbers, that soon India's southern beaches would look like slaughterhouses. No one knew, but now we are ready. Whatever natural disaster heads our way, we will stand together like the big, united country, we truly are. A wave has hit, yes, but maybe we're a little better off than before.

The End

SUNSET

sunset

Sunset. The magical barrier between night and day. The time when all barriers between fantasy and reality are severed. Colours streaming magnificently from the dying embers of the sun. All the world seems bathed in a golden light, still and calm. The golden sun sinks slowly down, until nothing is left but the fading colours which stain the sky.

Soon, little stars prick out like eyes. Twinkling merrily, they seem to be dancing. Pinpricks in the sky, they remind us how small Earth really is. The night sky looks like a deep blue velvet cape, soft and protective. A wind blows by, whispering unknown words. The moon rises, full and white. Like a face, it gleams, sending out rays of comfort and happiness.

I fall asleep, my head on the pillow of dreams.

The End

the DREAM

She saw the majestic creature rise up before her. Its coat gleamed white like the purest satin; its mane flowed like a waterfall. The tail streamed magnificently, but the horn outshone all. Lit by a warm glow, it shined like a beacon, changing colours. She longed to stroke that perfect head, to feel its satiny coat. She ran, and the deep blue eyes gazed into her, penetrating her, reading her. She stopped. Reaching to touch its coat…

Alyssa woke up. She shivered, remembering the vividness of the dream. Looking up at her ceiling, she saw the unicorns plastering it. But none of them came close to the awesome beast she had just seen. For Alyssa was certain that it was not just a dream. Something about it convinced her it was more…

Alyssa sighed. School today. How she hated school, especially when it got in the way of her trying to figure out something. Ah, well, at least it was a Friday. Alyssa sluggishly put on her clothes and tramped down the stairs.

School dragged by. Alyssa could barely stay awake. In the last period, (she was in 5th grade) her eyelids fluttered, and she fell into a deep sleep.

A moonlit glade surrounded her. The trees, washed silver by the moon, beckoned to her. A glassy, still pool was in the center. And emerging from it was he.

She knew it was a he. He called out in a language that was neither song nor words. But her heart tugged her onwards, and she slowly approached the beast.

Water streamed down his pearl white sides. The tail cascaded down from his rump. The flowing mane was gently pushed back by the light breeze. But to her, the only thing that existed was the luminous horn, with its wavering, dancing light, and the kind deep blue eyes. She walked on, following the blue gaze.

Suddenly, a scream tore itself from the unicorn's throat. His blue eyes wide with terror, he fled, leaves whirling. She cried out beseechingly, "No, please, don't go…"

"No, please, don't go!"

The math teacher looked oddly at the pale girl with black hair in the third row. Her brown eyes opened, and pain was imprinted there. The teacher felt shaken, but sternly called out, "Miss, if I catch you sleeping in class one more time, I will send you to the principal's office!"

"Sorry, sir," Alyssa muttered. She sighed wearily. If only she was at home!

Walking home from school that day, Alyssa felt strangely hot, even though it was winter. Philadelphian winters are brutal, but Alyssa was sweating by the time she got home. Her mother immediately felt her forehead, and was surprised to find that it was burning! Alyssa was put to bed straight away, and the doctor came to inspect her.

"I'm afraid she's got a severe case of malaria," the doctor said gravely. "Tell me, have you visited Asia within the last few months?"

"Yes, we were in India visiting a friend of mine last month, but you said that Alyssa had already had her malaria shots," her mother said.

The doctor consulted a file in his briefcase. He gasped. "Oh, Mrs. Sunn, I made a mistake! Alyssa had her malaria shot 5 years ago! Oh, dear!"

"Can you save her, doctor?" Alyssa's mother asked. The doctor looked into her pleading eyes and said heavily, "No, Mrs. Sunn, I cannot."

He came again. His coat shone in the early morning sun. He whinnied, calling her. The horn shone iridescent as she ran, butterflies flitting around her. She saw him crowned in a halo of golden sun, lifting his head proudly. He pawed the ground, and she was stunned by his gloriousness. Each eye cut through her, and saw into the love in her heart. And with one last whicker, he vanished…

Alyssa sat up, breathing hard. The doctor had left. Her mother sat at her bedside, but did not have the heart to tell her daughter the horrible news. So instead she said brightly, "Honey, you've just got a bad fever, and you'll be staying home for a few days. Okay?"

Alyssa nodded weakly. Her father came to sit in her room, and so did her two brothers William and Harry. They all looked at her gently, lovingly, until she fell asleep again.

The unicorn gleamed at the end of the meadow. She ran to him, floating above the grass. Birds sang joyous songs of spring, and butterflies danced like little sparkling jewels. She fell to the ground at his feet.Small flowers sprung up from the ground. She looked deep into his blue eyes, and only two words were said.

"Alyssa."

"Jewelhorn."

Jewelhorn bent his head, and she stroked it. The skin was silky and smooth, with not a single flaw. His horn shimmered, rainbow light dancing within it. Jewelhorn knelt, and she swiftly mounted him. She saw below her, in the grass, her parents and brothers surrounding a bed where a pale, sickly child lay. She whispered a goodbye to them. Then Jewelhorn galloped, and she sped away, up and up, until she was in the sky, dancing with the sun and moon…

Alyssa Sunn never woke up again. Her family distinctly heard a "Goodbye," echoing through the room as Alyssa took her last breath. Then she was still, never again to be bothered by worldly problems. Her mother wept, drenching her only daughter with tears. Her father sat stonily, as though not believing it was true. Her brothers caressed her pale face.

It was found that Alyssa had caught malaria on the last day in India. The virus was given time to mature, and became fatal. But the doctor seemed to think that Alyssa had simply given up the will to live. In truth, her longing to stroke the unicorn and ride it devoured her. In the end, she rode away on Jewelhorn, away from the earth and towards immortality.

The End